THE BOY AND THE SEA

THE BOY AND THE SEA

Orna Gadish

ISBN-13: 978-1977988263

ISBN-10: 1977988261

Library of Congress Cataloging-in-Publishing data:

Gadish, Orna
The Boy and the Sea

ISBN 1977988261

Manufactured in the U.S.A.

Once there was a sea...

And he loved a little boy.

And every day the boy would come,

and he would play in the water,

and swim,

and ride on the waves,

and run on the shore.

And he would fill his bucket with golden sand.

And they would build sand castles.

And when it was too hot,
the boy would go for a dip and cool
himself down.

And when the boy was tired,
he would fall asleep in his little boat.

And the boy loved the sea very much.

And the sea was very glad.

But time went on.

And the boy grew older.

The boy did not come to the sea.

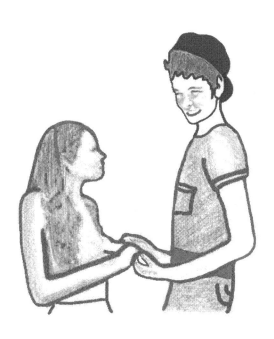

And the sea missed the boy very much.

Then one day the boy came back.

And the sea said: "Come boy, come and play in my water, and swim, and ride on my waves, and run on my shore, and build sand castles, and be cheerful."

"I am too big to play in the water and build sand castles in the sand," said the boy. "I would like to study and get smarter, but I don't have money."

"I am sorry," said the sea. "I have no money. But I do have plenty of fish.

Catch my fish and sell them in your town. Then you'll have enough money to pay for your studies."

And so the boy cast a fishing rod in the water... many times...

And he caught as many fish as he could.
And then he took away all those buckets
filled with shiny fish to his town...

And the sea was very glad.

But the boy did not come to the sea for a long time...

And the sea was often lonely and sad.

And then one day the boy came back.

And the sea was so excited that he cried tears of joy.

And the sea said: "Come boy, come and play in my water, and swim, and ride on my waves, and run on my shore, and build sand castles, and be cheerful."

"I have no time to ride on your waves or run on your shore," said the boy.

"I must work hard to earn a living.
I want to support my family and kids.
I need more money."

"I am sorry," said the sea, "I can't give you money.

But I do have plenty of sea products.

Come dive into my water and you'll be able to find some oysters, and clams, and scallops, and seashells, and corals, and pearls...

Take my sea treasures with you, sell them in your town, and become richer."

And so the boy dived underwater, and took away all the treasures of the sea he could find and sailed away...

And the sea was very glad.

But then, again, the boy did not come to the sea for a long, long time...

The boy was busy with his family and kids. He had his own house and his own company. He was very rich, but did not have time to visit the sea.

And then one day the boy came back.

And when he came, the sea was so thrilled, he was wavy and choppy.

"Come my boy," said the sea with a shaky voice. "Come and play in my water, and swim, and ride on my waves, and run on my shore, and build sand castles and be cheerful."

"I am too old to play in your water, too weak to ride on your waves, and too tired to run on your shore," said the boy.

"All I want is to thank you for what you gave me. Thank you, sea," said the boy.

"Is there anything else I can give you?" asked the sea.

"No," said the boy. "I have it all. Thank you."

But the boy was old, sad, and tired, and the sea saw it.

"Cheer up!" said the sea to the boy.

"I can give you something else!"

The sea was bubbly and smiled. "Step into my water and take a deep look down."

And so did the boy. He stepped slowly into the water... And he looked down into the sea...

And he saw his own reflection
looking back...

And the sea was very glad.

The End.

Made in the USA
Middletown, DE
14 May 2019